Sir Gadabout
Goes Barking Mad

D1151261

Martyn Beardsley

Sir Gadabout

Goes Barking Mad

Illustrated by Tony Ross

Dolphin Paperbacks

First published in Great Britain in 2005
as a Dolphin Paperback
by Orion Children's Books
a division of the Orion Publishing Group Ltd
Orion House
5 Upper St Martin's Lane
London WC2H 9EA

5 7 9 10 8 6 4

A catalogue record for this book
is available from the British Library

Printed in Great Britain by Clays Ltd, St Ives plc

ISBN 1 84255 275 9

www.orionbooks.co.uk

For Sonam, Shamoan and Amarah

Contents

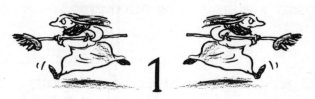

1

To The Willow Woods

A long, long time ago – long before you could send pictures from mobile phones, there stood a mighty and magnificent castle called Camelot. It was so mighty and magnificent that it would have had its own website – but it was well before those existed, too. The castle stood in a mysterious and misty corner of England, now long forgotten by all but the thousands of people who go to Cornwall on holiday every year.

Camelot was the home of the famous King Arthur. He was in charge of the Knights of the Round Table, and known throughout the world for his wisdom, bravery, and

1

collection of stamps from every country in the world (except Australia – which he was eagerly awaiting to be discovered so that his collection would be complete).

Arthur's queen was called Guinevere. She was renowned for her kindness, beauty, and fully-equipped workshop at the back of the Camelot stables. Here, knights brought their armour to be repaired, bikes to be fixed, and plans for fitted kitchens to be built.

On this particular day King Arthur and

Queen Guinevere were sitting regally on their thrones, which is what kings and queens spend most of their time doing, when a visitor arrived. A gangly knight in badly-fitting armour approached their thrones. He was struggling along with a small uprooted tree in his arms. The tree would have been heavy enough on its own, but to make matters worse there was a small girl sitting in it, clinging to one of the branches and shrieking to be let down.

The knight finally stood before the king and queen and bowed. As he did so, the tree tipped forward and the girl fell out and landed in Guinevere's lap.

"I want my mummy!" she wailed. (The little girl, not Guinevere.)

And when the front of the tree had dipped down, at the other end the roots tipped up violently, catching the Master of the Queen's Wardrobe under the chin. The blow launched him into the air, where his collar got caught on a chandelier. He swung helplessly in circles while still trying to appear dignified – as the Master of the Queen's Wardrobe must do at all times.

"I've got it, your majesties!" gasped Sir Gadabout – for it was he. Some said he was the Worst Knight in the World. Some called him other things – but those were even less kind, and we won't go into that.

"I see . . ." said King Arthur. "But, er, got what?"

"The tree! But I'm afraid it's not a round one like you wanted. And the girl didn't really want to come. Actually, her mother attacked me with a lethal weapon, but we got it all sorted out in the end."

(In fact, the girl's mum had beaten Sir Gadabout in a joust – where you charge at each other with lances – using  only a sweeping brush.)

"That's very interesting," said Guinevere. "But what made you bring them to us?"

"Why, your majesty – I got the message this very morning from Herbert's brother

Stanley. I was to bring you a round tree with a girl in!" Herbert was Sir Gadabout's squire – a sort of knight's servant. His brother was, well – just his brother.

Since neither the king nor queen could recall expressing a desire for a round tree with a girl in – not recently, anyway – Herbert's brother Stanley was summoned for an explanation. Stanley soon arrived, but when he saw what Sir Gadabout had delivered he shook his head.

"No, no – *that's* not what I said! Herbert told me to tell Sir Gadabout to 'bring a round tree for the king and queen from *Merlin*,' not '*with a girl in*'!"

A smile spread across Guinevere's face. "I think I'm beginning to understand ..."

Herbert was summoned. He was short and stocky, and fiercely loyal to Sir Gadabout.

"No, no, sire!" cried Herbert to his master. "It was: 'Bring Merlin to the king and queen at around three'!"

"Ah!" exclaimed King Arthur. "Now, I remember saying *that*!"

Guinevere chuckled quietly to herself. "An easy mistake to make. Now we've got it all sorted out, Gads, would you mind bringing Merlin along for us?"

"Right away, your majesty," replied Sir Gadabout. But instead of setting off, he stood shuffling from one foot to the other, looking rather puzzled.

"Anything else, Gads?" asked the king.

"Er, do you want me to bring Merlin *and* another round tree?"

"No, Gads …"

"Ah! Right! Just Merlin and a girl, then . . ."

Herbert pulled a funny face and pretended he was interested in a fly that was crawling up the back of Stanley's neck.

It all went rather quiet, and Sir Gadabout felt lots of eyes on him. "I'll go now," he said quietly, and slunk away.

Sir Gadabout and Herbert headed for the great wizard's cottage. As they ventured deeper into the Willow Wood, they kept their eyes peeled and their wits about them. (Herbert was better at the 'wits' part – but

Sir Gadabout could be very good at peeling his eyes.) They didn't want to get caught out again by Merlin's notorious guard-turtle.

When they got to the garden gate they saw a sign nailed to the gatepost with an arrow and *All Visitors This Way or Else* scrawled on it.

"That handwriting looks familiar ..." mused Herbert.

They followed the arrow on the sign, which led them to the rear of the cottage. Blocking the path to the back door was a large square panel of wood with a circular hole in the centre. Above it, a sign said: *Security Scanner. Place Head In Hole. Mind Your Fingers.*

"Hmm," said Herbert. "I'm not sure I like the look of this ..."

But Sir Gadabout was already thrusting his head into the hole. "It's the only way we'll get in, Herbert. I wonder what –"

At that moment there was a blood-curdling cry of, "*BURGLARS! OFF WITH THEIR HEADS!*"

Sir Gadabout twisted his head upwards just in time to see Dr McPherson the guard-turtle swishing a sword towards his neck with an almighty downward swipe. Sir Gadabout screamed like a tiny tot who has had his lollipop stolen, and was just wondering how he would be able to eat his breakfast without any mouth to put it into, when he felt himself being yanked backwards out of the hole by Herbert, who had quickly grabbed hold of his trousers.

Dr McPherson's sword missed Sir Gadabout's head by a whisker. The sword smashed
into the stone path below with a sickening
CLANG!! and sent a thousand vibrations
running up the turtle's arms. He fell on his
back with his sword-arm still shuddering so
violently that his shell rattled on the path
like a machine gun until it finally fell off
altogether.

"Another day in the life of the great Sir
Gadabout!" chortled a cat-like voice. It was
Sidney Smith, Merlin's sarcastic ginger cat,

who had come to the back door to see what was going on.

He stood with his arms folded and surveyed the scene: Dr McPherson's shell was rattling along the path towards the cabbage patch, and the turtle was wandering around dizzily, looking very pink and naked. Herbert was lying on his back with Sir Gadabout's trousers in his hands, and the great knight himself was adjusting his boxer shorts, which depicted scenes from Kings Arthur's Silver Jubilee celebrations. (The elastic had gone and they were held up by a bit of string.)

"Er, did I pass the security scan?" he asked.

11

2
Morag and Demelza

"I'd been expecting you to come for me!"
declared Merlin the renowned wizard when
Sir Gadabout and Herbert entered his gloomy
cottage, full of cobwebs, bubbling potions
and gigantic dusty books of spells.

"Oh," said Sir Gadabout. "Did you gaze
into your crystal ball and see a great knight
and his squire approaching?"

"A great fool and his nincompoop, more
like," muttered a cat-like voice from under
the table.

"No," said Merlin. He tapped his calendar.
"It's on here – today I go to Camelot for the
Magic World Cup!"

"*The Magic World Cup!*" gasped Sir Gadabout and Herbert together. It was one of the most important and exciting events imaginable (this was in the days before *Pop Idol*). The most powerful wizards, warlocks and assorted other magicians from all over the world gathered at Camelot in a battle of spells to see who was the greatest – and Merlin was the current World Champion.

It was then that Sir Gadabout and Herbert noticed that Merlin wasn't wearing his usual long flowing robes and tall pointy hat. He wore a purple tracksuit (covered in silver stars and moons). In one hand he held his kit bag, which had a magic wand sticking out of one end, and in the other he had one of those sports drink containers – but his contained some kind of brown, smelly, frothing liquid. It looked like he was taking this seriously.

They all set off for Camelot in great excitement. Sidney Smith was taking Merlin (whose memory was not what it used to be) through a checklist of things he should have brought with him. Sir Gadabout was trying to get the Camelot Wave going – but Herbert wasn't joining in, and a one-person Wave just wasn't the same somehow.

Along the way, they came across two rather odd looking men.

"Programmes!" said the first one, waving a glossy brochure under Sir Gadabout's nose. He was rather short, very scrawny, had a large hooked nose with a wart on the end, and a beard that seemed to have clear sticky-tape at the edges. His voice was strangely husky, and he, like the other, wore a white pointy hat with *Official Programme Seller* on the front.

"Only three groats!" said the other man, rattling a tin with money in under Merlin's nose. This man looked not unlike the first one.

"I'll take two," said Merlin eagerly. "There's probably a big picture of me some-where – they always do that for the champ-ion, you know!"

But Herbert was worried. "Those voices sound familiar to me ..."

"You've never seen us before in your life, shorty, so shut it!" snapped the first man.

"We're from miles away – the Great Barrier Reef or somewhere like that. So don't give me any of that 'familiar voice' garbage!" croaked the other man angrily.

In fact, they both shouted so forcefully that their beards began to slip off and they had to quickly press down on the sticky tape to keep them in place.

"Er, our whiskers are very weak ..." said one.

"They fall out easily due to a tragic childhood illness ..." said the other.

"I'll have *three* programmes!" Sir Gadabout cried, unperturbed by their weak whiskers. "They probably have big pictures of the great knights in there, too!"

"Yeah – so why are *you* buying them?" asked Sidney Smith.

Instead of passing a programme to Merlin or Sir Gadabout, the first odd looking man opened it up and blew on some silvery dust that was inside. Merlin, Sir Gadabout,

Sidney Smith and Herbert were all enveloped in a dusty cloud, and began sneezing uncontrollably.

When the air had cleared, Sir Gadabout said, "I – I don't know where I am or what I'm doing ..."

Now, with Sir Gadabout that was a pretty common situation. But when first Merlin, and then the other two also started saying similar things, the two odd looking "men" began to cackle in high-pitched voices.

"Success!" shrieked Morag.

"Once we've got Merlin out of the way, WE shall be World Champions!" cackled Demelza.

For these were the two wicked witches whom Sir Gadabout and co. had encountered before in their adventures. They tore off their white pointy hats to reveal *black* pointy hats concealed beneath.

"Quick – let's get Merlin away from them before the dust wears off," Morag urged.

"But who are we?" cried Sir Gadabout helplessly. "What are we to do?"

"I dare say your job will be to find Merlin!" laughed Morag evilly.

"Who is Merlin? Where can I find him?"

At that moment, a big slobbery bulldog wandered by. (He had run away from his owner after a bitter argument over whether to watch *EastEnders* or *Coronation Street*. The bulldog thought *EastEnders* was a bit depressing.)

"There!" cried Morag, pointing at the dog. "That's Merlin!"

"That's Merlin!" Sir Gadabout repeated as the dog waddled round a corner. "We must go after him!"

3

ARRR!

"It's Merlin, I tell you," said Sir Gadabout, patting the dog on the head (while at the same time it was dribbling goo from its mouth onto his shoes).

"Merlin is a tall man with a pointy hat," said Sidney Smith. "That is a slobbery fat thing with four legs and a tail, and it is called a 'dog'. It is *not* a human being, you clumsy clown."

"Ah!" said Herbert. "But a clown has got a red nose and big feet, so —"

"It just said something!" interrupted Sir Gadabout, peering closely at the dog. "I'm sure it's trying to talk to us!"

Like all bulldogs, the animal was indeed making lots of noises as it breathed in its wheezy, gruffling way – some of which sounded like words.

"Really? And what exactly did it say?" Sidney Smith asked Sir Gadabout.

"Well, it sounded like: *shmoodle*."

"Oh, well – that *proves* it! Only humans go around saying *shmoodle*, after all ..."

"But what if it's a spell?" Herbert wondered. "I feel really weird, and I can't remember anything that's happened during the last ten minutes or so. What if someone put a spell on us – and turned Merlin into a dog to stop him from winning the Magic World Cup?"

"That's it!" Sir Gadabout cried. "I feel strange, too!"

"You *are* strange," muttered Sidney Smith.

Sir Gadabout looked into the dog's eyes. "ARE – YOU – MERLIN?" he shouted.

The dog had a good scratch behind one ear, at one point during which he seemed to say, "*Arrr.*"

"There! It *is* Merlin!" exclaimed Sir Gadabout.

Sidney Smith clapped a paw to his head. "Good grief . . ."

"We have to find a way of getting rid of this spell – to Camelot, men!" cried Sir Gadabout, giving the dog another pat.

"*Arrr*," said the dog.

* * *

Meanwhile, Morag and Demelza, who had blown the last of the magic dust into Merlin's face to keep him under their spell, were leading the great wizard as far away from Camelot as possible and trying to find somewhere to dump him.

The first place they came upon was the village of Much Sniggering, and outside the village hall they saw a poster which said:

TODAY!
PRIZE VEGETABLE COMPETITION
judged by
ALAN TITTLEMARSH!

Morag looked at Demelza, and Demelza looked at Morag. "That'll do," they said.

Morag gazed deep into Merlin's eyes.

"This is the Magic World Cup. The people in there are all fools and won't believe you – but you must take no notice of them."

"They just want to stop you from being the champion wizard," added Demelza.

"For your first bit of magic," said Morag, "I should produce a giant marrow out of thin air if I were you."

As they propelled Merlin through the doors

of the village hall, he was mumbling to himself, "They're all fools … This *is* the Magic World Cup … Giant marrow …"

Morag and Demelza scarpered, and Merlin entered the village hall, where lots of people were milling around tables laden with vegetables: looking for the longest leek, the biggest onion, the orangest carrot, and so on. Merlin was met at the door by the famous Alan Tittlemarsh, who was as big in the world of gardening as Merlin was in the world of spells.

"Ah, a newcomer," said Mr Tittlemarsh, holding out his hand. "Pleased to have you with us!"

"You are a fool," replied Merlin, shaking his hand. "This *is* the World Cup."

"Oh, well, sort of . . ."

And then the magic dust wore off. Merlin was shocked to find himself in a room full of cauliflowers and cucumbers – but he had a vague memory that this was definitely the Magic World Cup, and that he had to produce a giant marrow to win it, despite all

these fools. (Wizards aren't often called upon to produce large vegetables, so it wouldn't be as easy as you might think.)

Merlin decided to check out the competition. There was a man wearing a battered straw hat and puffing on a pipe, standing proudly beside his entries for the Reddest Radish category.

"Most impressive," said Merlin. "What were they before you changed them? Toads?"

"No, seeds," replied the man.

"Very clever," Merlin nodded approvingly. "I'm entering a giant marrow."

"Where is it?"

"Oh, I haven't started it yet."

The man gave Merlin a funny look and took an extra long puff on his pipe. "Took me years to produce these!" he said, pointing at his radishes.

"You need a new wand," replied Merlin sagely.

At the next table Merlin found an elderly woman displaying her entries for the Fastest Runner Beans.

"How do you do," said the elderly woman. "We, er, don't get many people here wearing purple tracksuits with moons and stars on them ..."

Merlin shook her hand. "How do you do, you fool," he said, smiling kindly.

"Well!" she exclaimed indignantly.

"You're an old witch, aren't you? I can always tell!"

The elderly woman began to splutter and turn purple.

"*You ... I ... I've never been so ...*"

"May I borrow one of your runner beans?" Merlin asked, opening his kit bag and rummaging for his spell book. "I'm going to try and turn it into a gigantic marrow."

The woman hurried away, still purple and spluttering, to report the incident to Mr Tittlemarsh himself.

4
RUFF!

"It's Merlin, I tell you!" said Sir Gadabout, patting the dog on the head while at the same time dabbing its mouth with a tissue. He had bought a box of paper hankies to stop the drool from going all over him.

King Arthur looked closely and stroked his chin. "Looks like a bulldog to me, Gads."

The flabby animal was waddling around, gasping and grunting and slobbering everywhere.

"What's this you say about a spell?" asked Guinevere.

Sir Gadabout proceeded to explain to their royal highnesses what had happened to them

– as far as they could remember – on the journey to Camelot.

"I wouldn't have thought anyone could outwit a great wizard like Merlin," said King Arthur.

"I think we must have been taken by surprise," said Herbert. "*Something* definitely happened because I still feel a little woozy, too, your majesty."

"There!" exclaimed Sir Gadabout. "And I bet Merlin does, too. MERLIN!" he shouted, getting down on his hands and knees to look the dog in the eye. "HOW – ARE –YOU – FEELING?"

"Dogs aren't deaf," Sidney Smith pointed out.

The dog seemed more interested in sniffing around King Arthur's leg than answering the question. The king edged away, and Sir Gadabout repeated his question: "HOW – ARE –YOU – FEELING?"

"*Ruff!*" said the dog.

"Proof!" yelled Sir Gadabout, jumping to his feet. "Proof at last!"

"Hmm . . ." said Guinevere.

"Well," said King Arthur, "the competition starts soon and the other wizards are warming up. If that's not Merlin, you'd better find him. If it is Merlin, you've got to find a way to change him back quickly. I'm determined that Camelot isn't going to lose its World Champion."

Guinevere turned to Sidney Smith. "You've picked up a few spells during your years with Merlin – do you think you could change him back?"

"That would be much too difficult, your majesty," the cat replied.

"We don't *need* to!" beamed Sir Gadabout.

Sidney Smith groaned. "Look out – he's got a plan . . ."

"*I* shall disguise myself as Merlin! With the help of the real Merlin – and perhaps also a little from Sidney Smith – I'm confident that we can win the Magic World Cup!"

"But wouldn't that be cheating?"

"Not really, your majesty – since the *real* Merlin," said Sir Gadabout pointing at the dog, which was rolling on its back with its legs in the air, "will be doing the magic! You'll help us, won't you, Merlin?"

"*Arrr,*" said the dog.

No one could come up with anything better, so Sir Gadabout's plan was put into operation.

They entered the competitors' warm-up area, where they observed the Wild Wizard of West Lothian being put through his paces by his personal trainer. There was a half-cat, half-dog which he had created out of two separate animals and was furiously chasing itself in circles. And he was currently in a

frenzy with his wand, turning a row of pot-noodles into signed pictures of one of those boy bands. It was so effective that a crowd of screaming girls appeared and tried to snatch the pictures.

At first, the Wild Wizard thought the screaming girls were coming to see him, but when he realised they were only after the pictures, he became rather grumpy and turned the pictures back into pot-noodles.

The girls went away disappointed, but at least with something to keep them going till lunchtime.

"That's pretty good," yelled the personal trainer at the Wild Wizard. "But you can do better – gimme ten more pots, on my count!"

"Oh, dear," said Herbert. "He looks good."

"With Merlin's help, we shall beat him!" declared Sir Gadabout.

"With Merlin's help we might," grumbled Sidney Smith. "But with that slobbering mutt all we're going to get is laughed into the middle of next week."

They went somewhere quiet, away from prying eyes, to see what sort of spells they might be able to cook up between them-selves.

"I can *nearly* remember a simple spell Merlin used to do with trees," pondered Sidney Smith looking at a nearby oak tree. "If it's autumn, as it is now, you can change the leaves to look as though its summer.

Now, how does it go ...

Winter's coming, the year is old
Big Oak all covered in red and gold
Go back to summer, to the time
we've seen
When Oak was younger and his
coat was...

I just can't remember the last bit!"
"The previous line was 'seen', so its got to
end in 'een', I'd say," Herbert pointed out
helpfully.

"Merlin will tell us!" said Sir Gadabout. He gave the dog a playful tweak of the ear – which happened to be one of the things it *really* hated.

"*Grrr* –" said the dog.

" – *EEN!*" cried Sir Gadabout. "Merlin says the last word is 'green'!"

Sure enough, they were able to transform the tree into its full summer splendour, and they decided that this would be the spell they would use in the first round of the competition.

First though, Sir Gadabout had to disguise himself as Merlin ...

5
ARF!

In a large field beneath the towering walls of Camelot, thousands of people had gathered to see the Magic World Cup. Some wore face paint in the colours of their favourite magician, many wore scarves and hats in the same colours. Of course, it wasn't long before the Camelot Wave got going – and it was much more spectacular than when Sir Gadabout had tried to do it on his own.

The World Cup was to commence when King Arthur cut the golden ribbon across the gap in the fence around the field, where the competitors would make their entrances.

"Ladies and gentlemen!" King Arthur announced grandly.

There was a burst of applause from the spectators. There's nothing really worth applauding about the words "Ladies and gentlemen" of course – but the crowd were fed up with waiting so they were just glad something was happening at last.

"I now declare the Magic World Cup –"

He paused and turned to Guinevere. "Scissors please, my dear!"

"But I gave them to you!" Guinevere whispered.

"I don't think you did, my dear ..." King Arthur whispered back.

The crowd decided to clap again, hoping that it would please the king and hurry him along a bit.

King Arthur patted all his pockets. He found a pencil, a stone shaped like the Eiffel Tower which he'd found only that morning, a bit of money, and a digestive biscuit (although the patting had turned it to crumbs). But no scissors.

"Oh, I'll just have to use my teeth again like last year," he whispered to Guinevere.

"I now declare the Magic World Cup well and truly –"

He bent down and bit the golden ribbon. It was a very tough ribbon. The king gnawed and gnashed, but the ribbon wouldn't break.

"Is he having his dinner?" someone from the crowd asked.

"I don't know, but it's making me feel hungry," said another.

"Not us," said the girls who had had the pot-noodles.

"My dear . . ." whispered King Arthur in a strange voice.

"What's the matter now?" Guinevere asked. "Everyone's waiting!"

"*It's stuck in my teeth. I can't pull it out.*"

Two royal servants finally saved the day by untying each end of the ribbon from the fence posts. There was a loud fanfare from the Royal Trumpeters, and King Arthur finally finished off his announcement.

"… WELL AND TRULY OPEN!" The golden ribbon fluttering from his mouth as he spoke seemed to make the announcement even grander.

The crowd cheered, the first wizards appeared, and King Arthur slipped away to visit the dentist.

The first bout was between Mighty Mungo the Mountain Man, a surprise qualifier from the Himalayan Group play-offs, and The Great Mysterio, an unlucky semi-final loser at the last World Cup. (There had been a great deal of controversy over a refereeing decision. I could try to explain what it was all about, but the offside rule in magic is much too complicated to go into here.)

It turned out that Mighty Mungo the Mountain Man was a wrinkly, spindly little chap with incurable hiccups which ruined his spells. Allowances could be made in the qualifying rounds – but of course this was the Big One. The Great Mysterio merely had to make time go backwards for a few minutes to clinch a place in the next round.

It was then announced that the current champion, Merlin, was on next. There was a great roar from the crowd, and they all strained for a glimpse of the world-famous wizard.

When they saw him, the cheering crowd became quieter, saying, "Oh ..." and then, "Hmmm?"

The figure was as tall as Merlin, and wearing Merlin's great black cloak. But his face was hidden within the deep hood, and he had a strange shuffling walk which was not at all like Merlin's long loping strides. And a fat, slobbering bulldog trotted by his side, whereas the crowd felt sure Merlin owned a cat, not a dog.

In fact, Sir Gadabout – well aware that he wasn't as tall as Merlin – was sitting on Herbert's strong shoulders under the cloak. And Sidney Smith, who would have to play a big part in helping with the spells, was hidden up one baggy sleeve. He was having to hang on with his claws, making Sir Gadabout's eyes water.

Their opponent was Alfonso, from Spain. Luckily for "Merlin", Alfonso was only a part-time wizard. He was actually a road sweeper from Madrid and had only got this far because his opponent in the qualifying stages had caught the 'flu. Rumours that Alfonso himself had caused the illness with a sneaky spell could never be proved.

The crowd cheered once more as "Merlin" strode towards an oak tree in the middle of the field.

"I will now make this tree and all its autumn leaves appear to be in full summer bloom!" announced Sir Gadabout in his best Merlin voice.

The crowd said, "*Oooh!*"

"*How does that rhyme go?*" Sir Gadabout asked Sidney Smith. Luckily, the crowd thought that talking up his sleeve was part of Merlin's spell.

Sidney Smith whispered most of it, but as before, forgot the last word. Sir Gadabout wasn't worried – he could always ask the dog. He began to chant:

Winter's coming, the year is old
Big Oak all covered in red and gold
Go back to summer, to the time we've seen
When Oak was younger and his coat
was ... was ...

Sir Gadabout thought hard, and scratched his head (giving Sidney Smith a good old shake in the process). Then he looked down at the dog for advice.

"Arf!" slobbered the dog.

Half!

cried Sir Gadabout triumphantly.

The tree instantly began to change – but instead of blooming with green leaves, it stayed stubbornly autumnal. However, before the crowd's very eyes it shrank to half its normal size!

Those in the crowd who thought it was supposed to happen shouted, "*Hurray!*" Those who knew it wasn't shouted, "*Eh?*"

It was hard to tell whether the judges would mark the spell as a flop or a clever trick.

Fortunately for Sir Gadabout, Herbert and Sidney Smith, Alfonso came out next and made their job much easier.

His act started badly. He came into the arena at a sprint, but as he went past "Merlin" he tumbled to the ground, claiming he had been deliberately tripped. The judges decided that this was a dive, and told him sternly to carry on with his wizardry.

Alfonso announced to the crowd what kind of spell he would be performing: "Ze beautiful lady, I turn her into ze donkey!!!"

Out into the arena came his assistant, the lovely Marguerita, wearing a bright red dress covered in sparkling sequins. She was dragging a large, heavy sack behind her.

"In ze bag, ze beautiful lady carries hay for when she is ze donkey!"

"*Ooooh!*" cried the crowd.

"I've never seen anything like it!" said someone.

"It appears that Merlin's crown as World Cup Wizard is wobbling!" said another.

The noise *almost* drowned out what

sounded like a lot of *eeyor*-ing coming from the sack of hay. The beautiful Marguerita clambered into the sack, and Alfonso waved his magic wand over it and said some strange words.

It seemed as though a fight was going on inside the sack, with a lot of bulging and billowing – and what this time *definitely* sounded like *eeyor*-ing.

Out popped a donkey – wearing a bright red dress covered in sparkling sequins. Alfonso bowed to the crowd, but they were not impressed, and began to boo him.

The judges had had enough and rushed to

the sack. They were just about to pull out the beautiful Marguerita when they realised she was no longer wearing her bright red dress with sequins, so they left her inside. The crowd booed once more (although I'm not sure why this time).

Thwarted, Alfonso began to utter some strange, angry words in the direction of "Merlin", and Sir Gadabout began to sneeze violently. But before it could turn into the 'flu, the judges dragged Alfonso, the donkey, and the sackful of the beautiful Marguerita out of the arena.

Merlin was declared the winner!

"That was against a total fraud!" groaned Sidney Smith from up Sir Gadabout's sleeve. "There's no way we can get any further!"

"My shoulders are about to give way!" warned Herbert.

They hurried from the arena.

6

The Dog Food/
Cat Food Spell

Sir Gadabout, Herbert and Sidney Smith had slipped away to a quiet spot behind the arena where all the magic was going on. They had heard that their next opponent was to be Marcel le Marvellous, the wizard to the King of Gaul and thought by many to be as good as Merlin himself.

Even Sir Gadabout was beginning to get worried. "Are you *sure* you can't turn the dog back into Merlin?" he asked Sidney Smith.

"I am! For one thing, I don't know a powerful enough spell. And for another thing,

THE DOG IS NOT MERLIN AND NEVER WAS!"

"You believe it's Merlin, don't you?" Sir Gadabout said, turning to Herbert.

"Well ... I suppose ... I mean ..."

"See!" said Sir Gadabout.

"Er, and even if he isn't," continued Herbert, "couldn't you think of a spell to swap him for Merlin anyway?"

Sidney Smith sighed. "I could *try* – but it might go horribly wrong."

"Try! Try!" cried Sir Gadabout.

"Well, there was a spell I learned for turning dog food into cat food – Merlin sometimes picks up the wrong tins from the supermarket. I suppose I could change the words a little and see if it works."

"Yes!" said Sir Gadabout. "I'll just get ... Where's Merlin?"

Merlin – or rather the bulldog – had disappeared while they were talking. They all started rushing round calling and whistling and talking loudly about biscuits and bones, but he was nowhere to be found.

"I don't know why I bother!" complained Sidney Smith to Sir Gadabout. "First you lose the real Merlin, then the dog that's supposed to be him!"

While they were searching, they heard a commotion going on in the royal enclosure, where all the important people were watching the World Cup.

They rushed to see what was happening, and arrived in time to find King Arthur – who had returned from the dentist's having

had the golden ribbon removed from his teeth – flat on his back with the bulldog standing on his chest. To make matters worse, the dog was ravenously pulling at King Arthur's clothes and gulping down everything he could get off.

"Very sorry, your Majesty," said Sir Gadabout. "In all the excitement I suppose we forgot to feed him."

"I quite – *URGH*!" spluttered the king. The dog had polished off his outer Royal Robe, but before it started on the Royal Vest it decided to give the king a nice slobbery lick on the lips to show there were no hard feelings. "I quite understand – but do you think you could get him off me?"

"What? Oh, yes!" replied Sir Gadabout. "Although I'm not sure he's finished yet . . . "

The dog turned its attentions to the Royal Vest, and the nibbling began to tickle the king's tummy so much that he couldn't talk for laughing. Sir Gadabout assumed that King Arthur was enjoying himself after all, and left the dog to his lunch.

In the end Herbert managed to step in and get the dog away from the king. By this time his stomach was gurgling and grumbling alarmingly, and he was burping every few seconds (the dog, not the king).

They got the animal back to their quiet spot, and Sidney Smith took a few deep breaths and prepared himself for the spell. It took some time, since the rumbling and burping coming from the greedy dog kept putting Sidney Smith off. But finally, he raised himself onto his hind legs, gazed into the dog's eyes, and began to recite his own version of the "Dog Food into Cat Food" spell:

By the power of all
That is wise and fair
This tin of, er, bulldog
Must disappear
And in its place
let there be
A tin of Merlin
For all to see!

All eyes were on the dog.

For a moment, it stopped gurgling and burping. It stood stock still, its eyes staring straight ahead in a very odd way. Then its body began to change shape! It stretched, it squeezed, it turned, it twisted, until it had turned into –

A tin.

The dog's head and tail remained the same, but its body, although still covered in fur, was now the cylindrical shape of a can of pet food.

Sir Gadabout scratched his head. "I don't recall Merlin looking quite like that . . ."

Herbert went up to pat the dog – which was looking pretty worried and gurgling and burping more than ever.

CLANG! went Herbert's hand as it struck the dog's back.

"Well, I *said* it might go horribly wrong," sulked Sidney Smith. He hated being in the wrong, and he dashed off to find some mice to chase instead.

Sir Gadabout and Herbert heard an announcement from the arena.

"*Will the next contestants – Merlin and Marcel le Marvellous – make their entrance for the first semi-final!*"

"*Eeek!*" said Sir Gadabout and Herbert together.

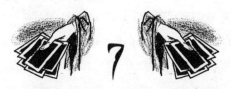

The Great Card Trick

"*Eeek!*" said Sir Gadabout and Herbert again.

Sidney Smith was nowhere to be seen and there wasn't time to find him. They looked at the tin-shaped bulldog. Its stomach – full of King Arthur's chewed up clothes – was still rumbling, though now in a very tinny, echoey way.

But with the crowd waiting, they had little choice other than to quickly get into their Merlin disguise and enter the arena.

Marcel le Marvellous was the first to perform. To get himself warmed up, he gathered lots of stones from around the field, and with a wave of his wand turned them into bars of chocolate, which he handed out to the crowd. This got a great round of applause. Then he performed his main spell.

He planted a single seed in the ground, uttered some special words, and waved his hand over the seed in mysterious patterns. The seed immediately began to grow, until the most beautiful flower anyone had ever

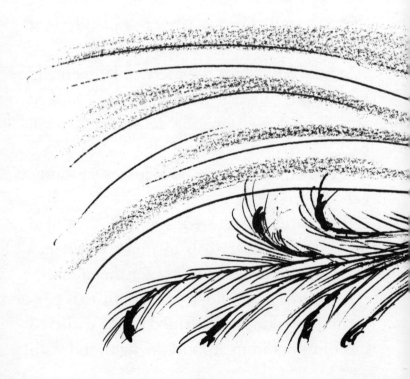

seen blossomed before the eyes of the on-lookers.

The crowd began to cheer – but that wasn't the end of the spell. Suddenly, the red petals of the flower began first to tremble, then move up and down rapidly like wings. In an instant, the flower turned into a magnificent bird, which soared into the sky and began swooping and circling around the arena.

The crowd began to cheer again – but *that* wasn't the end of the spell. The bird hovered close to the ground at one end of the field, then suddenly shot high into the air leaving a dazzling rainbow behind it. And when the rainbow was complete, the bird vanished in a flash of white light.

The crowd by now weren't sure whether it was time to cheer or not – but when Marcel le Marvellous smiled and bowed, and with the rainbow still hanging over the arena, they got to their feet and clapped and called for more.

"I wonder if we can beat that," Sir Gadabout said as he wobbled on top of Herbert's shoulders.

"With a fair wind and a bit of luck, sire," replied Herbert pluckily.

Sir Gadabout looked at the tin bulldog, gurgling, burping, and wobbling around unsteadily on his little bandy legs. "It's just a matter of coming up with a spell ..."

Just before they went out to face the crowd, Herbert had an idea. "I know a card trick, sire! You get someone to pick a card, put it back into the middle of the pack – but when they turn the top card over, it's *their* card!"

"Excellent!"

"The last time I tried it, it didn't work out quite right …"

"Er, fairly excellent, anyway."

They managed to borrow a pack of cards from a mate of Herbert's, then strode out into the arena. The crowd were excited. Marcel le Marvellous had performed some amazing feats of magic – but surely the great Merlin would come up with something even better!

"For this extraordinary feat I require a volunteer from the audience," Sir Gadabout announced. A man with a runny nose came forward. From under Sir Gadabout's great cloak, Herbert whispered the words he should say.

"*Shuffle the cards and then give them to me.*"

But instead of saying it, Sir Gadabout shuffled the cards and then reached inside his cloak and offered them to Herbert. Both the man with the runny nose and the crowd were mystified as to why Merlin should stuff the card inside his cloak where no one could see them.

"*No! Say it!*" Herbert whispered again.

By now, the man with the runny nose was getting worried. He knew wizards were different – but he could have sworn that this one had a voice coming from its stomach.

Sir Gadabout eventually shuffled the cards, asked the man to pick one and memorise it, then return it to the pack. The trick was that when he opened the pack for the man to put his card in, Sir Gadabout was to sneakily peek at the card above it – he would then know that the card he was looking for followed that one.

The trouble was, Sir Gadabout was never very good at remembering all those different coloured funny shapes and numbers . . .

"And your card was . . ." He looked through the deck slowly and carefully. The crowd began to grow restless – this wasn't exactly the kind of amazing magic they had expected from Merlin.

"THE SIX OF DIAMONDS!"

The crowd cheered.

"Nope," said the man with the runny nose.

The crowd sighed.

Sir Gadabout went through the cards again. "Could have been an upside down 'nine' I suppose," he mumbled to himself. He pulled out another card.

"THE NINE OF DIAMONDS!"

The crowd cheered.

"Nope," said the man with the runny nose.

The crowd sighed.

"Shall I give you a clue?"

"Not yet," replied Sir Gadabout, going through the pack once more.

Then he clumsily dropped the whole

pack, and the cards went fluttering in all directions.

The crowd started to go home for dinner.

But somewhere in the crowd were two women. They were disguised as car park attendants – even though there were no cars in those days it was still better than revealing their true identities.

For they were Morag and Demelza – the two witches who had caused all this trouble in the first place. They had entered the competition as the Delightful Doreen and her cute assistant Dolores – and in fact they had just beaten the Great Mysterio in the semi-final.

"Ha-ha!" cackled Morag. "The plan has worked. Merlin's out of the way, and *we* shall win the World Cup!"

"But wait," cautioned Demelza. "What if we help the mad knight to win this one? That way, we get to face him in the final – which would be a *lot* easier than trying to beat Marcel le Marvellous."

"By Jove, you're right!"

Just as the crowd were turning away, Morag began to utter some strange words in a deep and husky voice. At the same time, Demelza waved her hands in special patterns – and the spell began to work.

All the cards that Sir Gadabout had dropped on the ground began to rise by themselves. As they floated upwards, they slowly gathered together until they had formed the shape of a bird with gracefully flapping wings. It looked exactly like the one that Marcel had produced – except this one was twice as big. And it flew around like Marcel's – but twice as fast. And at the end of the performance it turned into not one rainbow, but a hundred, filling the sky with multi-coloured light.

"How did we do that, Sire?" whispered Herbert from beneath Sir Gadabout's wizard cloak.

"Perhaps I *can* do magic after all!" beamed Sir Gadabout proudly.

"And I'm a butcher's dog," remarked a cat-like voice from the sidelines.

In fact, neither Morag and Demelza themselves were really powerful enough to perform a spell like this – they had sneakily pinched it from Marcel's book of spells many years ago.

Nevertheless, there was now no doubt that "Merlin" was the winner. Marcel was hopping mad, because it seemed to him that Merlin had stolen the very spell he had intended to use in the final. But it was too late. The crowd cheered and got ready for the final, and Marcel le Marvellous stormed off muttering some very non-magical words (fortunately in French).

And so it came to the moment everyone had been waiting for – the final of the Magic World Cup!

The Grand Final

There was a lot of razzmatazz before the main event. Even though it all gets rather boring and everyone just wants to get on with it, it's just something you have to have before a grand final.

For example, the crowd had to stand through the national anthems of both competitors and the country which was holding the competition. Since everyone was from England and it was being held in England, this meant the same anthem had to be gone through three times, with polite applause between each one.

"I thought the second anthem was the

nicest," Sir Gadabout commented. "Which country was that from?"

King Arthur was about to leave his seat to get the final underway, when a group of his soldiers rushed by.

"What's the matter?" he asked.

"Trouble at the prize vegetable competition in Much Sniggering, your majesty!" the sergeant replied.

"Oh, dear. What is the world coming to? Better get along then."

King Arthur proceeded to introduce the two finalists to the crowd (fortunately there were no ribbons to be cut this time) and then the contest was underway to find the greatest wizard in the world.

The Delightful Doreen and her cute assistant Dolores – known to you and me as Morag and Demelza – were to go first. They decided to use a spell they had stolen during a quiet moment at the last World Cup from Montague the Magic Mule (who was so good that many people had suspected he was not a mule at all but a wizard who had turned himself into one) (which actually was correct, but the truth was never revealed) (until now, by me, of course) (I hope you can follow what's going on in all these brackets).

The spell entailed making a little group of trees on the far side of the field uproot themselves and dance a waltz around the arena. The thinnest branches of the trees became violins and bows, which played the music to which the trees danced.

This was pretty spectacular and impressed the crowd. But because the spell had been stolen from a mule, the only way Demelza and Morag could make it work was to pin tails to their bottoms and waggle them about while chanting the words.

The judges hastily consulted the rule books to see if there was anything that said you couldn't waggle your bottom in a public arena. There wasn't, and Morag and Demelza were awarded very high marks indeed.

"*Now* what are we going to do?" asked Sir Gadabout as all the trees gave three low bows, then cart-wheeled back to where

they'd come from to thunderous applause.

"We could run away while there's still time," suggested Sidney Smith. "Besides, if you want to do something useful you ought to be taking that dog to a vet!"

The poor animal was by now gurgling like a blocked drain.

"He does look rather green," Herbert admitted.

"We can't miss the final!" Sir Gadabout

cried. He turned to the dog. "Please give us a spell we can use to win the final," he begged.

The dog continued to gurgle in a tinny sort of way – and Sir Gadabout convinced himself that it was saying, "*Juggle a bubble and loop the loop.*"

"Of course!" said Sidney Smith. "All we need are some bubbles and a flying machine and we're World Champions!"

"We can at least make a start with the bubbles," insisted Sir Gadabout. "I'm sure you could magic up some of those!"

And before long, Sir Gadabout found himself standing in front of an expectant crowd with a bag of bubbles in his hand.

One of the problems with this idea was that Sir Gadabout didn't know how to juggle – not with balls, clubs, elephants or bubbles. But he'd seen it done lots of times and thought it looked pretty simple . . .

Unfortunately, a bit of a breeze had been building all day, and the crowd laughed when Sir Gadabout threw the first bubbles

into the air and they sailed high into the sky before he could grab them. This went on for some time. Herbert was doing his best to run around so that Sir Gadabout could chase the bubbles. But this meant that Sir Gadabout, sitting on his squire's shoulders, was having difficulty keeping his balance. The sight of the magician staggering around the field chasing bubbles, waving his arms around and bending strangely at the middle made the crowd roar with laughter.

Sir Gadabout accidentally bumped into the dog, and a hollow CLANG! echoed around the field. The dog began to choke and splutter, and within seconds had coughed up all of King Arthur's clothes (and felt much better for it). The king insisted vociferously that the Royal Golden Tights did *not* have those holes in them before the dog got hold of them, despite all the rumours.

"A magic dog!" cried the crowd. "Made the king's clothes appear from nowhere!"

Sir Gadabout clung on desperately as Herbert hopped about on his good foot while he clutched the one which had kicked the tin dog. "*Ooooh!*," cried the squire. "*That's tough tin!*"

"He's doing a talking-stomach spell – amazing!" cheered the crowd.

What with the breeze and the hopping around, what they had feared all along finally happened – the deep hood which was hiding Sir Gadabout's true identity fell backwards, revealing his face to everyone.

There was a gasp.

"He's turned himself into a nutty knight!"

"HE'S NOT NUTTY!" warned Herbert.

"And there goes the stomach-talking spell again!" said the crowd. "What a performance!"

The crowd were so busy watching the amazing spectacle before them (and trying to pop the bubbles which were floating around their heads) that they did not notice a group of soldiers leading the real Merlin back to Camelot. But Merlin *did* notice that the World Cup – including someone disguised as him – was taking place without him.

"*That's not me!*" he protested. In the blink of an eye, he broke free from the soldiers and raced towards the pretend Merlin. With the soldiers stampeding after him, all the crowd could see was a cloud of dust heading towards the centre of the arena. (Of course, they thought it was a magical cloud of dust.)

When the dust had settled, Merlin was on his feet in the centre of the arena. Struggling furiously on the ground around him were Sir Gadabout, Herbert, Sidney Smith and the bulldog, wrestling with a group of soldiers.

"He just seemed to make them appear out of thin air!" marvelled the crowd.

There could be no doubt about it – Merlin was still the World Champion Wizard!

"And I'm also the Much Sniggering Prize Vegetable Champion," declared Merlin at the banquet held afterwards to celebrate his victory. "But I seem to have, er, upset one or two people, and I believe they are changing the rules to prevent wizards from entering in the future."

"It takes more strength than you realise to carry Sir Gadabout on your shoulders all that time," said Herbert. "But I think I could have gone on a bit longer if those soldiers hadn't knocked me over."

"I somehow felt my mental powers making those cards rise into the air and swoop around the arena!" said Sir Gadabout. "I'm thinking of writing a book on how to develop your magical ability."

"I'm thinking of writing a book on how to avoid being driven mad by nutty knights," grumbled Sidney Smith.

And everyone knew, deep down, the answer to whether or not Sir Gadabout was still the Worst Knight in the World –

"*Arrr!*" said the dog.